PRINCE SPARROW

BY MORDICAI GERSTEIN

FOUR WINDS PRESS

New York

10 9 8 7 6 5 4 3 2 1

The text of this book is set in 13 pt. Palatino.
The illustrations are line drawings with halftone overlays,
prepared by the artist for black, red, and yellow.

Library of Congress Cataloging in Publication Data
Gerstein, Mordicai.   Prince Sparrow.
Summary: When a sparrow flies into her room on her
eighth birthday, a mean and selfish princess, convinced
that it is a charmed prince, keeps the bird close to her.
[1. Sparrows—Fiction.   2. Birds—Fiction.
3. Princesses—Fiction]   I. Title.
PZ7.G325Pr 1983   [E]   83-11558
ISBN 0-590-07907-7

For my mother,

FAYE,

who was called

Faygeleh,

which means

Little Bird

Everyone thought the Princess was a brat.
"She's completely selfish!" they said.

She was mean and nasty to her maids.

She called them awful names.

She was rude to her tutor, and she had terrible tantrums
when she didn't get exactly what she wanted.

Of course, no one would spank her or even scold her.
She was a Princess.
Everyone prayed she'd never become Queen.

At her eighth birthday party her father, the King, was
called away.
"It's royal business, my dear," he said as he hurried out.

The Princess had her worst tantrum.
She smashed all her presents and threw them at her guests.
Toys and dolls and jeweled music boxes crashed on walls
and went flying out windows.

"Now clean up this mess!" she ordered her maids
   when she was finished.
"And you, Tutor! Read me a fairy tale!"
   She loved stories about magic and enchantment.

"I'm going to be a witch when I grow up, so I
   can turn you all into toads," she said.
   The tutor sighed.
"Once upon a time," he read, "a witch enchanted
   a Prince, changing him into a little wild bird—"
   But here, the tutor was interrupted.

There was a whir of wings, and a sparrow flew
through the window and into the Princess's room.

The maids screamed and waved their brooms.
The tutor covered his head with his book.
"It's the enchanted Prince!" yelled the Princess.

"Shut the window and be still!" she snapped.
"I'm going to catch him."
No one breathed while the sparrow fluttered
wildly around the ceiling.

When the bird settled down in a corner,
the Princess crept slowly toward him like a cat.
"Hello, little bird," she whispered.
"Are you really an enchanted Prince?"
The bird watched her creep closer.
"Chirp," he said.

Suddenly
he leapt up,
chirping fiercely.
The surprised Princess
tumbled backwards.
"Stupid bird!"
she screamed.
"I'll get you!"
The sparrow
chirped back at her
from the ceiling.

Finally, with a bit of bread, the Princess
coaxed the bird to the back of her chair.
From there the sparrow looked her over,
turning his head this way and that.

She had never been looked at so boldly
before. She saw he was small but fierce,
and she knew that he wasn't afraid of her.

"I think you are an enchanted Prince," she announced.
"Prince Sparrow shall be your name!"

Prince Sparrow remained perched on her chair. He spent
the night with her in her room.

In the morning the Princess ordered the royal silversmith to make a little silver cage. When it was ready, she put seed and water in it.

Prince Sparrow hopped all around it.
Then he looked at the Princess.
"Go in," she said. "It's nice in there."

Prince Sparrow went in, and the Princess locked the door.

She jumped when he shrieked and hurled himself
against the bars. He beat them with his wings.

"You stop that immediately!" the Princess commanded.
But he didn't stop. The cage rocked. "You'll tear yourself
to bits!" she cried. At last she opened the door, and
Prince Sparrow flew out in a burst of feathers.

"When you get hungry," shouted the Princess, "you'll have to go into your cage for food!" Prince Sparrow flew to her chair and seemed to glare at her. He perched there all day.

That evening as the Princess ate her strawberries
and cream before bed, the sparrow fluttered down.

He landed on the Princess's spoon and helped himself to a strawberry.

"Those are my strawberries!" cried the Princess.

Prince Sparrow chirped back at her and took some more.
The Princess laughed. She had a sweet laugh.
"This bird is a Prince!" declared the Princess. "From now
on he must be treated like one!"

From then on, Prince Sparrow ate with the Princess.
He came and went in the palace as he pleased. He dozed on the Princess's shoulder while she did her schoolwork and went for rides with her in the royal carriage.
He splashed in her bathtub and then dried himself on her hair.
"You're the only sparrow in the world that has a Princess for a towel!" she said.

At night he nestled beside her on her pillow,
and she told him all her secrets. Prince Sparrow
became her first and best and only friend.
A year passed quickly.

The day before the Princess's ninth birthday, she found Prince Sparrow flying round and round her room. He flew to the window and pecked at the glass. His sad, wild cries frightened her.

"What's wrong?" cried the Princess, but she thought she knew. "You don't want to leave me, do you?"

Prince Sparrow flew to her and
chirped in her ear. "No," said the
Princess, "I won't let you go!"
Prince Sparrow threw himself
against the window and beat
on the glass with his wings.
The Princess tried not to hear.

At last she opened the window.
"Please stay!" she said.
For a moment Prince Sparrow
perched on her shoulder.
Then she felt and heard the whir
of his wings. He was gone.

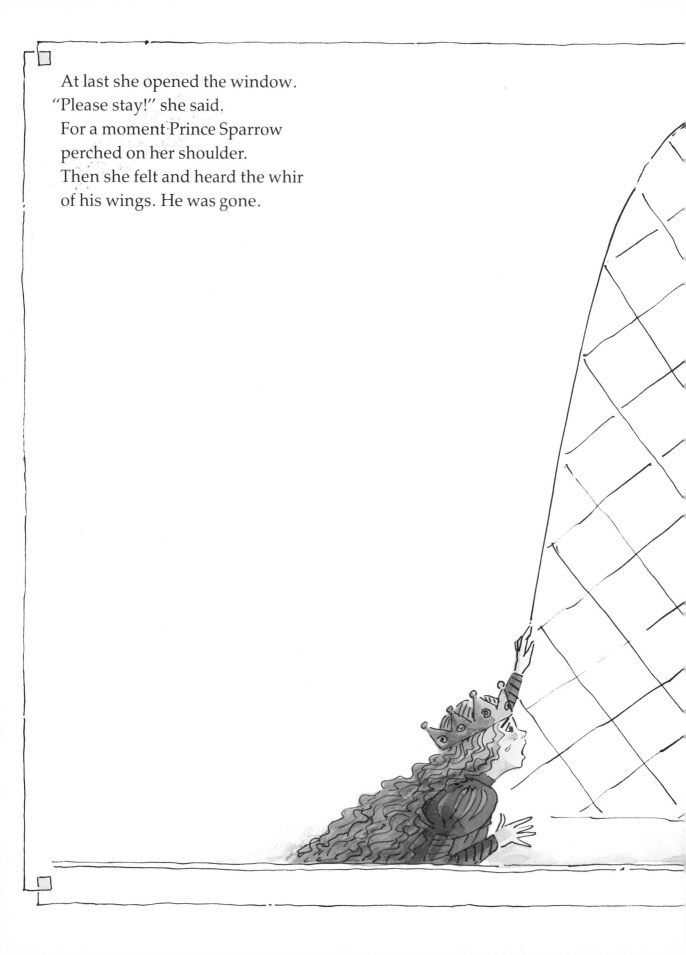

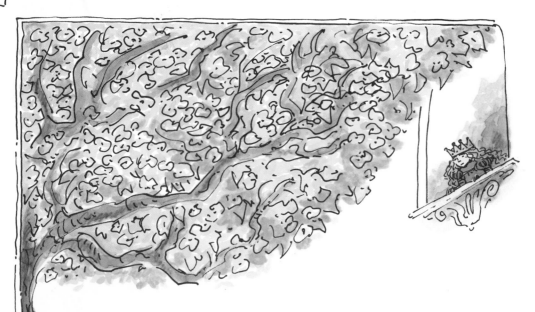

Through her tears the Princess looked out the window. It was spring; there were sparrows everywhere. They were courting and building nests and filling the air with their raucous chirping. They all looked like Prince Sparrow.

That night
the Princess dreamt
that Prince Sparrow
came back to her.
In her dream he changed
from a bird into a real Prince,
and the Princess began to cry.
"Why are you crying?"
asked the Prince. "You
gave me my freedom and
broke the spell. Now I
can grant you any wish!"
"I loved you as a sparrow!"
wept the Princess.
"Chirp!" said the Prince.

"Chirp! Chirp!"
  The Princess awoke and sat up.
"Prince Sparrow, you've come back!" she cried.
"You're just a sparrow after all!"

Prince Sparrow never left again. For the rest
of his life he remained what he was, a sparrow.
The Princess grew up to be a Queen.